LITTLE
LOST
TIGER

BY JONATHAN LONDON

ILLUSTRATED BY ILYA SPIRIN

MARSHALL CAVENDISH CHILDREN

Text copyright © 2012 by Jonathan London
Illustrations copyright © 2012 by Ilya Spirin

Marshall Cavendish Corporation
99 White Plains Road
Tarrytown, NY 10591
www.marshallcavendish.us/kids

Library of Congress Cataloging-in-Publication Data
London, Jonathan.
Little lost tiger / by Jonathan London ; illustrated by Ilya Spirin. —
1st ed.
p. cm.
Summary: Amba, a Siberian tiger cub, is separated from his mother by a
forest fire in the Siberian wilderness.
ISBN 978-0-7614-6130-2 (hardcover) — ISBN 978-0-7614-6131-9 (ebook)
1. Siberian tiger—Juvenile fiction. [1. Siberian tiger—Fiction. 2.
Tigers—Fiction. 3. Animals—Infancy—Fiction. 4. Forest fires—Fiction. 5.
Siberia (Russia)—Fiction.] I. Spirin, Ilya, 1976- ill. II. Title.
PZ10.3.L8534Lgt 2012
[E]—dc23
2011021909

The illustrations are rendered in watercolor, pastel, and gouache.
Book design by Anahid Hamparian
Editor: Margery Cuyler

Printed in Malaysia (T)
First edition
1 3 5 6 4 2

mc Marshall Cavendish
Children

For Sean, a young tiger,
with thanks to Peter Matthiessen & John Haines,
poets of the wilderness

—J.L.

For Nikolai

—I.S.

AS THE WINTER SUN SINKS
into the Siberian wilderness,
the Striped One steps silently
across the alder flats,
certain of what she seeks.

In her tracks bounces Amba
like a huge, playful kitten.
He is hungry.

A river in its icy bed
mumbles in its sleep.
The wooded hills and ridges
sparkle with snow.

Shaggy and frost-tipped,
the tigress and her cub
slip like shadows into a forest
of bone-white birches.

The Striped One sprays her scent
and marks her territory with her claws.
A dark-eyed Ural owl
hoots and blinks in the frozen night.

In a moon-bright forest clearing,
three sika deer in thick winter coats
nibble the stubble and twitch their ears,
listening for danger.

Quietly, quietly,
the Striped One nudges Amba
beneath a fallen tree . . .

then stalks on big, silent paws
through the deep snow.
She must get close without being sensed—
or Amba will go hungry.

Creeping low, the Striped One
glides through the moonlight,
floating like mist.

Moon shadows of tree trunks
streak the snow
as the Striped One crouches
and gathers herself,
ready to pounce.

Suddenly there's a *ROAR*—
louder than any tiger's.
It's the wind.
And with the wind . . .

Fire!

Flames leap,
ignite the tree crowns, lick the moon.
Sparks dance, pop, *hisssssss.*
Amba squeals for his mother.

Hares and sables and wild boars
bound across the flame-lit snow.

The sika deer spring from their clearing.

The Ural owl spreads his great wings
and takes to the sky.

The Striped One's eyes flare up,
and dagger-like teeth
gleam in the firelight.

With a loud grunt, she calls Amba—
then leaps through the trees
like a tongue of fire.

Out, out, into the open alder flats,
the Striped One tears through a marsh
of tall, dead grass . . .

out to the middle of the frozen river.

There she stops and gazes back,
her eyes blazing in the night:
  Mother tiger burning bright
  in the forest fire's light.

But where's Amba? Her little one?
The Striped One roars—

AA-OOOONH! AA-OOOONH!

But no cub comes.

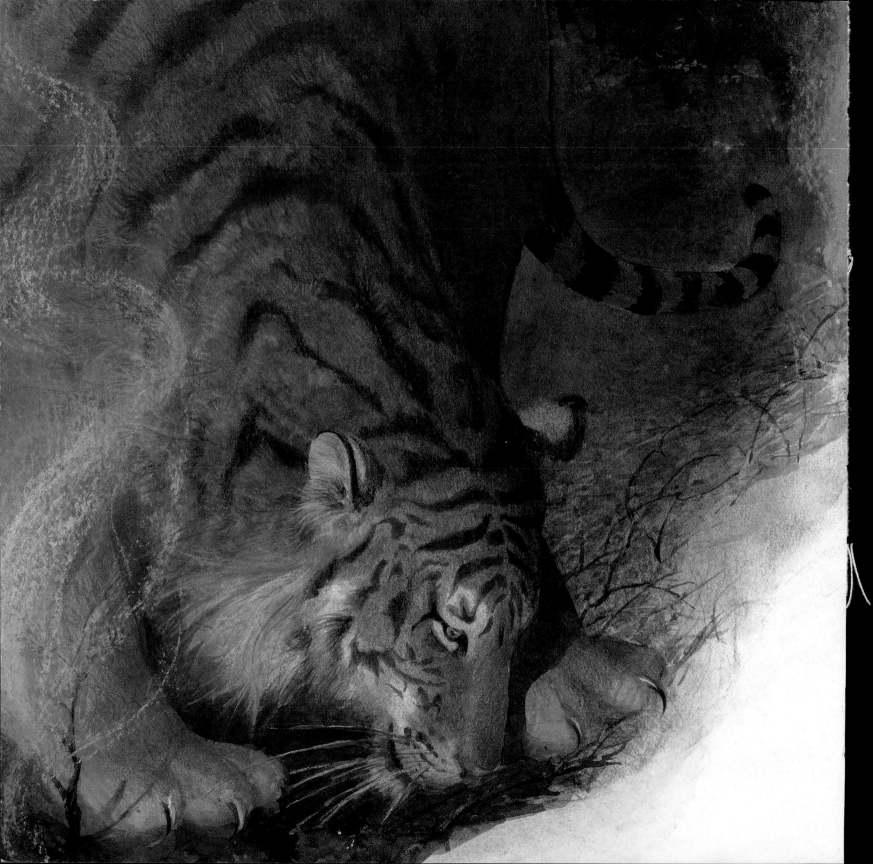

All night, the Striped One roars and searches,
clawing downed fiery limbs,
sniffing the wind.

In the morning, the world
awakens. The wind has died—
and with it, the fire.

Across the icy stillness,
a distant cry can be heard.

Miiaaaow! Miiiaaaaow!

And Amba—
    leaping from a hidden cave—
comes running.

The Siberian tiger is the biggest cat on Earth. Males can weigh 800 pounds and can stretch 10 feet from the nose to the tip of the tail. Tigers are among the most endangered species on Earth. They have been hunted to the brink of extinction. In 1947 hunting of the tigers was banned, but poaching has continued. Many of the tigers are killed for their body parts, sought after by the Asian medicine market. Others are lost to logging, which ruins the tiger's habitat. If humans don't protect wild habitats, there will be no tigers left in the wild. There are now only 350 to 400 Siberian tigers in the forests of eastern Siberia.

Siberian tigers are solitary hunters, roaming territories of up to 600 square miles. They prey mostly on deer, wild boars, and elk. They mate usually in late winter or early spring. Fifteen weeks later, one to four kittens are born blind in sheltered dens. They weigh 2 to 3 pounds. The mother is on her own, nursing and protecting her young and teaching them to hunt.

The Udege and Nanai tribes call the tiger "Amba," a sign of great respect. The young cubs live at high risk from large black or brown bears, but also from floods and forest fires. A cub may join her mother on a hunt at two months old, but it must be kept well hidden when the mother makes her final attack.

A hungry tiger can eat 60 to 100 pounds of meat in one night. But although Siberians can run 50 miles per hour, they catch their prey only one in ten times. They may have to walk more than 30 miles a night looking for prey, using their striped coats for camouflage.

Naturalists are working hard to save the Siberian tiger so that "Amba," revered as the True Spirit of the Mountains, will not be lost forever. —J.L.